The U.S.K

Dedicated to all visible minority kids
who struggle with fitting in.

By Sophie Eruokwu

RASOPH PUBLISHING CANADA
Copyright © 2022 Sophie Eruokwu

ISBN: 978-1-7781112-1-1

Contents

Chapter 1

A Sad Beginning

Fourteen year-old Zora sat on the park bench, sighing with misery. The people who walked past her gave her funny stares and she did not like it. After moping for a few minutes, she decided to go back home and maybe take a nap or something.

The walk back home was just as bad as sitting on the bench. People stared and pointed at her, whispers floating in the air as Zora hung her head low, before finally getting home. She opened the door and took off her dirty shoes before waving at her dad, who was reading a newspaper in the kitchen. Work had been... difficult on him at times. Zora knew when he read the newspapers (which he actually hated to do), chances are he had a hard day at work.

As she went upstairs, she waved at her nine-year-old brother who was playing video games in the living room.

"Wanna play with me?" He asked her as he paused the game.

She shook her head with a smile. "Nah, I'm good. Besides, you look too far into the game to add me in. Thank you though." she said politely.

Her brother nodded but sighed a little after unpausing the game. Zora sighed a little too. Even though she was not in the mood to play video games, she felt bad for him. She knew her brother was pretty lonely in this town too; the kids at school were also hard on him. Playing video games was a form of escapism for him. But sometimes, he just wanted to share it with a friend or two. Just sometimes.

Zora finally got to her room, sat on her bed, and frowned. Why did her father have to take the new job? They were all happier back in her home country. Even though her father had a job here as a surgeon, it was obvious that his colleagues did not like him; with the exception of his boss, who admired his extraordinary skills.

Well, all he had wanted was 'a quiet life for his family', so he had accepted the job offer and relocated the entire family to this town that was in the middle of nowhere. It wasn't as busy and diverse as the big cities she had *expected* to move to. No, this place was too quiet, too secluded, and too de-meaning to people like her.

Her mother was trying to make the best of things in the new town by opening a confectionery store, just like she did back home. But business was not the same here: almost nobody came to her store in this town and it was obvious they did not want to.

And when it came to school here, it was far worse than expected. Her classmates

were quite mean to her and they did not in-
volve her in any fun activities. She did not
have many friends. Actually, she had none.
It was the same situation for her little
brother, who was also struggling to fit into
the new town. A tear fell from her eyes.
This was all because they were black. The
only ones in this entire town. "I wish we did
not have to move. I wish I still had friends...
I wish we didn't look so different!" she said
sadly as she continued to sob.

* * *

Zora woke up to somebody calling her
name from downstairs. As she hurried
down the stairs, she noticed that it was her
mother calling for her from the kitchen.

"There you are!" Her mom said, as Zora
walked into the kitchen. "It's already 1pm! I
know it's Saturday but that doesn't mean
you should waste the day sleeping." Her
mother shook her head as Zora reached for
some toast that was set for her on the table.

"Sorry mom," she said as she crunched noisily on the toast.

Her mother rolled her eyes. "Anyway, I called you down to help me run an errand; could you run to my store and pick up a few things? I think I put them in a green bag beside my office desk." Zora frowned. "Oh no, I planned not to leave the house until... Monday, for school. "I know you don't want to interact with anyone but I really need this stuff. I can't get it myself because I have a meeting to go to now."

Zora sighed as she got up. "Alright then, I'll just get ready first." Her mother smiled. "Thanks, sweetie! Here are the store keys." She handed her daughter the set of keys. "I need to run now but see you later — and thank you again!" she said before rushing out of the house. Zora waved goodbye before making her way upstairs to get properly dressed.

* * *

As Zora had expected, the numerous pairs of eyes descended on her once more, staring and whispering a multitude of things. The increasing volume of the whispers caused her to increase her speed. She tried to walk fast and turned down a road where her mother's store was located. She scrambled to the doors and frantically opened them with the keys. Once she got inside, she breathed a sigh of relief as she locked the door. She had made it!

She strolled past the counter of the confectionery store and opened the door to her mother's office. It was quiet and calm. The green bag was beside the messy desk, just as her mother had told her. She slung the bag over her shoulder and was ready to leave the store.

Then, she noticed something (or someone) right outside the glass doors of the store: her classmates! She ran behind the counter and peered at her chattering peers.

They always made fun of her whenever they got the chance and she definitely wasn't going to give them the opportunity to do so again.

She crept to the back of the store and opened the back door quietly before dashing out. Unfortunately, she must have alerted her classmates because soon enough, she heard shouting and footsteps following her. She then noticed she had been running with no clue where she was going and she had found herself in a field of yellow grass. A large, dilapidated house stood some distance away from her. It looked like a barn but also like a factory. Zora wasn't sure.

She had outrun the bullies but she needed a place to hide until she was fully sure they were gone. This rickety old building might do the trick! She had noticed, well, more like tripped over a small trap door not too far from the building; it was covered with dead weeds. With the green bag still tightly in her grasp, she pulled the trap door open and crept through it with no hesitation. Even though she was not fully inside yet, she heard a voice call out, "Hey! What are you doing here? "

* * *

Zora quickly got up to dust herself. She looked up and was amazed by the sight before her; homes, stores, and tall buildings all littered the place. However, it all seemed to be made of cardboard. Children of different ages were walking about and carrying out their daily business. As she marvelled at the cardboard city, the voice called out again.

"Hey you!" She turned her neck quickly and caught sight of an angry boy that was walking up to her. She also noticed that the boy...looked like her. He was also black. She quickly overcame her bewilderment and had to think of an escape plan. Zora contemplated whether to run or confront him. Where would she even run away to? Not to mention how tired she was from running anyway. "You're not supposed to be here." The boy said once he was in front of her. Too late!

"I was just... I..."

"Who are you anyway? And... how did you even get in here?" the boy asked, fuming. The other people in the cardboard city stared at them, curious about the intruder within the walls of their little home.

"Leave her alone, Kamau!" Another voice cried out before walking up to both the kids. She had a panicked look plastered on her face. She reached out to hug Zora and let go shortly after. She was also black.

"Ignore my brother over there." the girl said with a disapproving look at her twin. She turned back to Zora.

"Are you okay? Did those mean kids hurt you? " She said this with concern as she led Zora to a funny-shaped building that was plopped at the centre of the small city. Questions whizzed around her head. How did she know? And why was she so nice? Once they had reached the building, the three of them entered and Zora was awestruck by how stylish the inside was. Though it was still made of cardboard, it appeared regal. She sat down on a surprisingly comfortable couch and put down her mother's green bag. "I'm Keesha, by the way." the kind girl said.

Two kids burst into the room at the same moment. "Is it true? Is there really an intruder inside? " one of them asked as Keesha rolled her eyes.

"No, just a guest." She then pointed at them. "That's Anaya and that's Raheem." Zora awkwardly waved to them as they did the same back.

"But what is this place really?" Zora asked.

"Well, you're at the Underground Society of Kids! " Anaya cried out with glee.

"Or the U.S.K. for short," Raheem said.

"It's a place for kids and, well, orphans who are perceived... differently than others," Kamau said quietly. "We're the U.S.K. leaders, all four of us, and we live here in the town hall." Keesha said with a smirk.

"How...did you guys even get here?" Zora asked inquisitively.

"Well, a long long time ago-" Keesha started to say.

"Oh stop being overdramatic. It was like, 2 years ago. The town was a bit different from what it is now. All our families were on this large refugee ship, sailing to the big city for better 'opportunities' as our parents had said." Kamau said, scolding his sister.

"It wasn't the best experience, but we had each other and that was all that mattered." Raheem said with a sad smile.

"But on one dark night, a storm hit the ship, and the waves were pretty intense." Anaya said as she repeatedly twisted a bit of her hair.

"Yeah, all the kids were put on the lifeboats while the adults scrambled around, trying to make the ship steady, and also pack some things."

"That was when a large bolt of lightning hit the ship, and it knocked the lifeboats into the sea." Kamau said, folding his arms.

"Which we were all in." Anaya said.

"The ship, on the other hand, caught fire and sank...we all lost our parents that way; and we never saw them again." Keesha said as she cast her eyes downwards.

"So when we washed up to shore here, you could imagine how disgruntled the people were to see us." Kamau muttered.

"And we thought it was best if we went our own way." Raheem said with a shrug.

"Being the oldest kids, we had to lead the younger ones, and make a plan for survival." Anaya said with a proud smile.

"So ever since, we've been building this little home here; using parts from the city scrapyard mostly. Our parents had taught us many skills, thankfully, such as sewing, cooking, building, and other cool stuff. With these skills and the fact that the townspeople don't really care what they throw away-"

"You won't believe how much books, furniture and other stuff we find! It's like they only use them once and discard them!" Anaya said with giggles.

Kamau looked at her with a frown. "As I was saying, with these skills and the fact that the townspeople don't really care what they throw away, we managed to build a 'humble abode' for ourselves here." He said with a nod.

"All on your own? No adults?" Zora asked with astonishment.

"Yup! This place was built for kids, *entirely* by kids, and has been around for quite a while now." Anaya replied.

"We made this little city where we make our own clothes, grow our own food, and even teach the younger ones to read and write. Everyone has a skill that can benefit the whole U.S.K." Raheem said with glee.

"But what happens if you grow, like, really old? Too old to be considered a kid?" Zora questioned.

"Well...when that happens, you probably have to go to the outside world by yourself." Kamau responded.

"Like... banished?!" Zora asked with surprise.

"Oh my goodness, no! Maybe more like a farewell party." Keesha said quickly.

"Yeah, like wishing you good luck in the outside world." Raheem said.

"And not to the wretched town. No. Rather, you could probably go on the path opposite the town. We don't know exactly where it leads but we know that it could lead to a better life than the U.S.K. for a really big kid, and far better than this town; the big cities, you know, since that was where the refugee ship was heading anyway." Keesha said with a small smile.

The five children chatted for a while, until a loud alarm blared through the air.

Chapter 2

Show Time!

"More intruders?!?" Kamau cried out as the children got up. Keesha looked at a telescope that was positioned at the side of the room.

"Ah, it's those kids that were giving you a hard time, Zora." she said with a grin. Zora felt her heart stop at the mention of the bullies. Anaya smiled widely.

"Well, let's give them a lesson they will not forget." All but Zora grinned wide as they scrambled to the corners of the city hall, pressing buttons and pulling levers. Suddenly, an array of windy and ghostly noises emitted from the old factory.

"Leave here, don't look back, or you'll regret it!" Kamau said in a creepy voice into a mic. Zora stood there, confused at what was taking place. Keesha noticed and took her towards the telescope.

"Just take a peek from here." she said with a smirk. Zora looked through and instantly giggled, as she watched the bullies run (even faster than when they were chasing her!) "Stay away! Stay away!" Kamau screamed from the speakers.

As the antics came to a close, all of the kids burst out laughing.

"Oh my goodness, that was priceless!" said Anaya. "It has always been." Raheem said, still giggling.

"Not to sound like an idiot, but... what just happened?" Zora asked between chuckles.

"That was our defensive system, to drive away intruders." Keesha said as she sat on the couch.

"How come it didn't detect me when I snuck in the trap door?" Zora asked.

"Because I quickly turned it off as soon as I understood your situation. This means that, from now on, the alarm wouldn't go off at all when it recognizes your face. I knew you needed help and... it also seemed like you needed a friend or two." Keesha replied.

Zora frowned at the thought of her helplessness.

"Aw, cheer up! Why don't we take a tour of the city? You seemed intrigued by it." Raheem suggested.

Everyone but Kamau shouted with glee and rushed out to show Zora around. They went about, showing her all the wonders their little home could offer, filling Zora with amazement. While still on the tour, she realised what time it was. Her mother was expecting her! She quickly said bye and picked up the green bag before leaving. As she rushed out of the U.S.K. with a smile on her face and contentment in her heart, she picked up speed and raced to her home. Things were finally starting to look good.

* * *

It was now Monday. A school day. Zora was not happy at all. She dragged her feet while going to school. Kids stared at her with wide eyes and some stifling back giggles as she did things like get books from her locker or walk to a class. While her teacher was droning on about science and whatnot, Zora's head was in the clouds.

She was thinking about the U.S.K. She thought it was so cool that a bunch of kids lived in harmony and peace within such an unlikely place. Her thoughts got interrupted by a crumpled piece of paper that bonked her head. A nasty girl named Bree let out an annoying laugh.

"You should have seen the look on your face!" she said, still laughing. Zora tried to ignore her as Ms. Turner, their teacher, passed out sheets of paper that had instructions on them.

Ms. Turner said "alright kids, for your projects, I'm going to put you in groups. Martin, go with Jake and Lily. Peter, go with Tom and Tina. Zora, go with Bree and Poppy."

But Bree shook her head, "No, Ms. Turner! We don't want to have her in our group; she's not like us." she said with a frown.

At that moment, the bell for the end of the day rang, and Zora used this golden opportunity to bolt out of the class. She didn't want her classmates to see the tears forming in her eyes. She went past the courtyard, down the street, behind her mother's store and started to slow down in front of a certain broken-down factory building.

Visiting the U.S.K. again was sure to brighten up her mood.

* * *

"Try to forget about those losers." Anaya said, whacking a branch on the path they were walking on.

"They don't understand that their attitude towards people like you and us is just plain wrong." Keesha said, with a bite of an apple.

"Even if it hit them in the face." Kamau said, causing his friends to laugh. Zora managed to smile a bit. She and the U.S.K. were going to a nearby lake to spend the rest of the afternoon, mostly with the goal of cheering Zora up after her awful school day.

Once they arrived at the banks of the lake, some of the kids removed their clothes to reveal their swimwear underneath and quickly jumped into the pool.

Zora was given a spare swimsuit so she could join in on the fun. The kids laughed, played and splashed for hours before retiring back to the bank and just chatting as the evening sun dried their soaked bodies.

Zora liked this atmosphere. She liked being surrounded by people she could call friends. She liked being around people who looked like her. She especially liked being happy, with the feeling that she had not a single care in the world. She loved this feeling.

* * *

The five children were walking back to the U.S.K. building, all still chatting gleefully.

"We should get water guns next time!" Anaya said with glee. "Agreed!" the others said unanimously.

When they were inside the U.S.K. heading for the town hall, the alarm sounded. Keesha ran to her telescope and frowned. "It's those annoying construction workers!" she said angrily.

"Ugh! They're always lurking around here, wanting to demolish the abandoned factory!" Anaya hissed.

"Which is our only home..." Raheem said as he hung his head low.

Kamau smirked. "What are you waiting for?! Let's scare them out of their wits again!" he mischievously said. The others grinned as the same ghostly scaring procedure took place. Levers, buttons and spooky noises were pulled, pushed and made.

Zora peeped through the telescope and giggled. "They're running away!" The group of kids yelled a hurray before settling down on the couch or floor.

Raheem shook his head. "We may have done it now. But for how long will we do this?"

"Until I can get the golem to work." Keesha replied with a sigh.

"The what?" Zora asked curiously.

"The gole- oh yeah, you haven't seen it before." Keesha said as her eyes lit up. "Follow me!" she said excitedly before dashing upstairs, with the others following her.

In this new (and HUGE) place, machinery, tools and other great things covered the place, and at the centre, what appeared to be a giant robot sitting down there, motionless.

"Can this place get any cooler?!" Zora said with a laugh. Keesha giggled and went to a control panel.

She pointed to the robot made out of scrap metal. "That is the golem! Fireproof, waterproof and it can also act like a big metal suit with its own control panel!"

She pressed a button on the panel, and the robot's eyes glowed an eerie blue before it attempted to stand up. Unfortunately, it lost its balance and collapsed on the ground before shutting down, returning to its previous state.

"Keekee still needs to work out a few bugs, but after that, we'll have a perma-nent-" Kamau started to say.

"And efficient protector of the U.S.K.!" Anaya finished saying.

"Where did you even learn how to build stuff like this?" Zora asked with even more amazement.

"My dad was an engineer, and an awe-some one too. He taught me all I know about electronics and of course, robotics." She said with a smirk.

Zora looked back at the golem again, her eyes still filled with awe.

"It looks so cool!" Zora said, tapping the robot on its back.

"It would be cooler if it would actually work!" Keesha grunted as she kicked it.

"You've spent like four months trying to make this. Don't worry, you'll get there." Kamau said with a smile.

Before Zora could spend time being astonished at Keesha's skills, her eyes caught sight of the clock.

"OH MY GOODNESS! 7PM ALREADY! My family is probably worried sick about me! I have to go!" she cried before rushing downstairs.

"Bye guys!" she said, frantically waving at them. "Bye!" "See you soon!" and "Be safe!" were the replies that came back. Zora smiled. Those were definitely better than hearing "we don't want you here" or "you're not like us." Definitely better.

Chapter 3

The Good and Bad Times

From that day on, Zora was much happier; she loved her new friends and spending almost everyday with them. Sure, school still sucked and her classmates were annoying, and sure, her mother scolded every time she came back late from visiting her new friends (like when she came back at 7pm after gawking at the U.S.K's golem. Her parents never let her hear the end of that!) but the U.S.K. was something she looked forward to every single day.

Her new mood continually got the attention of her parents and her younger brother, who were just thrilled that she was not moping about the house. She even had sleepovers with the U.S.K. gang, sometimes indoors, other times outdoors, like camping.

She liked to sleep under the stars while she and her friends softly talked about the events of the day and what they were going to do the next day. Life was good and she wanted nothing — nothing at all — to change.

* * *

It was a sunny Wednesday afternoon and Zora was walking to the U.S.K. after school, as usual. With a skip in her step and a tune she was whistling, she strode through the town with her heart at peace.

That was when she noticed something odd. A little girl with red hair and a wide grin stood very close to a lake with a teddy bear. The stuffed bear was accidentally dropped in the lake but when the girl reached for it, she fell in too!

"Help! Help!!" She cried out as she struggled to stay afloat. Zora rushed into action and jumped into the lake.

"Hold my hand!" She cried as the little girl fearfully clutched onto her (and the stuffed bear she retrieved). Zora swam out of the lake and breathed heavily, as her soaked clothes stuck to her. The little girl coughed violently, before looking at Zora with astonishment.

"*You* save me?" The girl said with confusion as she looked at Zora doubtfully, like she could not believe that someone like Zora saved her.

"You SAVED me!" She cried out again but excitedly. She hugged Zora tightly before running off with the wet teddy bear trailing after her within her hand. Zora smiled before shaking herself in an attempt to get dry. She continued on her way and arrived at the U.S.K. where she told the others of what just happened.

"That's so cool!" Raheem said with glee.

"Such a heroic move!" Keesha applauded.

The others lauded her too but Zora brushed it off with embarrassment. "It's not that much of a big deal. I just thought it was the right thing to do." she said.

"You saved someone's life! How is that not a big deal?" Kamau asked with shock.

"I don't know. I was just... doing what anyone would do. No biggie." Zora replied with a chuckle.

* * *

It turns out it was actually a big deal. It turns out the girl Zora saved was Georgina, the mayor's (bratty) seven year-old daughter. And it turns out Zora was wrong. Very wrong. The newspapers were covered with articles about her and her heroic action, much to Zora's surprise. When she walked down the street, she still heard whispers but ones filled with wonder and admiration compared to the usual ones of confusion she often heard. But this wasn't the end of it. At school, she had *literally* become popular overnight! Everyone wanted to be her friend, everyone wanted her to sit beside them during lunch, everyone wanted her to be in their groups during projects. Zora was not used to getting this much attention. Even Bree saved her a seat in the cafeteria, beside two of her friends, Poppy and Juniper.

And it still doesn't stop there! Zora was interviewed by the mayor, who constantly thanked her for saving her 'precious little rose,' Georgina.

Zora's mom was getting in on all the action too; her store was flooded with customers now, compared to prior when she was lucky to get a person in a week.

It did really seem like things were changing and Zora kind of liked it.

* * *

It was a nice evening and Zora was in her mother's cafe with her friends. Well, her new friends Bree, Poppy and Juniper. They were chatting, giggling and snacking, and at that moment the back door of the store opened. It was Anaya and Raheem.

Zora almost choked when she saw them. She didn't exactly know why they were here, but she did not want to speak to them at that moment. Or any moment really — she didn't want them to embarrass her in front of her other friends.

"Zora! What's up?" Anaya said with a wave as Zora put her head down.

"We hadn't seen you for a while and we were worried." Raheem said calmly.

Bree looked at them with disgust. "And who are those?" she said with deep contempt.

"Uh, just some —" Zora began to answer but a sharp stare from Bree made her change her tone. "— um, some people that live around here."

Anaya was taken aback by her answer. "Zora, yo! We're your friends! Stop pretending!" she said with a nervous laugh.

"Uh, I don't really... know you guys." Zora said, turning her eyes from them.

"...What? You're joking, right?" Raheem said as sadness filled his voice.

"No, apparently she's not." Juniper said, flipping her hair; although her facial expression was portraying an emotion of guilt.

"So get lost." Bree said, folding her arms.

"Yeah!" Poppy chimed in with a giggle.

Anaya and Raheem couldn't believe their ears.

"Fine." was all Anaya said before she and Raheem slowly walked out of the room with their heads hanging low.

Zora felt bad. She felt REALLY bad. How could she have done this?

She sighed, and was about to go after them when Bree held her back.

"Don't follow them." She commanded.

"Yeah, you don't need them." Poppy said with a scoff, though Zora could notice a sense of regret in her voice. "You're one of us, and that's all that matters." Bree smirked.

As Zora sat back down, she felt the weight of the world fall on her shoulders. One of them... all that she ever wanted... right?

* * *

Zora tossed and turned in her bed that night. She still felt bad. Really bad. She kept replaying the scene in her head, and she felt worse each time she thought of Anaya and Raheem's shocked faces.

The whole thing happened so fast... and she just couldn't believe she said that she 'didn't know them.' She sighed as she got up, went to her window, and opened it.

A full moon was out and it illuminated the sky. It reminded her of how she and the U.S.K. spent time under the stars and moon when they went out camping. But that was a long time ago and unlikely to happen again. She went to her bed and tried to sleep. Maybe she would feel better, even the slightest bit, tomorrow.

However, that was not the case. In fact, that wasn't the case for several days. She was quite down and everybody saw it. It didn't help that her guilt was stopping her from visiting the U.S.K. too.

One day on a walk back from school, she decided to do something bold, something brave, and something that probably

should have been done earlier; She was going to apologize. Yes, apologize to her
U.S.K. friends.

This was very important. She picked up
her speed and ran as fast as she could to the
broken-down factory behind her mother's
store.

Chapter 4

Backfired

"What on Earth are YOU doing here?" Keesha said with a frown when she spotted Zora creep into the town hall. Zora jumped, then smiled sheepishly. Kamau followed his sister's gaze and also frowned at the sight of Zora. "Oh, you know... coming for a visit..." Zora said nervously. "Ha! You hadn't visited in like a month!" Kamau said with a scoff. Zora started to explain herself but Anaya interrupted. "It doesn't even matter." she said with a flip of her hair. "Do we even know you?"

Zora's mouth fell open. "Look, can I just apologize?"

"Oh really? Is your paparazzi here to get it on camera? Since you're so popular now?!" Anaya barked.

"Whoa, calm down. Please, let me just explain." Zora replied, waving her hands in defeat. "Sorry, we don't want to hear it since, you know…" Keekee began to say.

"Since we're not your friends." Raheem said in a sad tone.

"Would you guys just listen!?! LET ME EXPLAIN!" Zora said, starting to raise her voice.

"Whoa, you shouldn't be the one angry here. What about us!?! You abandoned us!" Kamau exclaimed.

"But you don't want to hear me out!" Zora barked.

"And of what importance is what you have to say to us? We heard you loud and clear; you've been accepted into the 'big leagues.' You don't need us." Keesha said with a shrug.

"Is that it?! Are you guys jealous?! You should be happy for me that I have a place in the city; I've wanted that ever since I moved here!" Zora yelled.

"So what are we then? What's the U.S.K. to you then? Goose feathers?!?" Kamau replied angrily.

Zora was now boiling with anger. "Maybe that IS true! Maybe I don't want you guys! You're just... not like me anymore! I have new friends now and you're not like us!" she screamed.

The four other children looked at her with shock as Zora stormed away from the town hall. The other children in the cardboard town looked at her with confusion as she navigated between them to get to the trap door and leave this place, for good.

* * *

Days went by. Zora did not visit the U.S.K. She was done with them; they couldn't even let her explain! She finally got what she wanted from this city but she lost her old friends! *Maybe it was for the better,* she thought. She mostly spent her time hanging out with Bree, Poppy, and Juniper to help her take her mind off the U.S.K. But no matter how much she tried, a deep hole was in her heart and she wasn't sure if it would ever be filled.

* * *

Smoke. Fumes. Heat. Everywhere. Zora leaped out of bed. Fire.

She flew to her window, and gasped at the sight. It was blazing close to her house, leaving a path of destruction behind it. How could this have happened?!? She flung open her door. Zora banged on her brother's room door before forcefully entering.

He was also awake with fear in his eyes as he stood in front of the window, watching the part of town closest to the forest lit ablaze.

Zora grabbed his hand and ran out of the room. At the same time, her parents rushed out of their room.

"Quickly kids, outside!" Zora's father cried out as the family hurried down the stairs. The living room was already catching fire and the family knew that they had to move fast. They bolted out the door, and looked at the destruction the flames were causing to, not only their home, but the neighbors' homes. "Everyone! To the town square! It's safest there!" Somebody on the street yelled. Many people who were also on the streets got into their cars. Others just started to run to the town square. Zora's family jumped into their car and started to head toward the town hall.

The two children watched the destruction from their windows as tears filled their eyes and fear filled their hearts. Once they arrived at the townhall, they joined the large crowd of people in their pajamas and sleepwear, all angrily and fearfully standing together. The mayor was also there, trying to calm her citizens.

Zora thought hard and long. She couldn't let this continue on. That's when her mind glossed over the thought of the U.S.K. golem. It was fireproof... maybe they could save some people or something with it. Maybe Keesha finished it (at least, that's what Zora hoped).

Now she just needed to escape her parents. She started to sneak away slowly, as her parents were involved in the town discussion about what the next move was, but someone tapped her shoulder. It was her brother!

"Where are you going Zora? Please don't leave me!" he pleaded. "No, I'm going to get help; I think I know how to stop this. Just stay here and don't tell mom and dad that I left. I promise it will all be better soon." she said, hugging her brother. He nodded, then started to cry and wave good-bye as she ran away.

When she got to the yellow field, she heard her name being called. "ZORA! Wait up!" It was quite dark, but the flames in the town illuminated their faces a bit. It was Poppy and Juniper! "We wanted to follow you!" Poppy said.

"Yeah, we noticed you leaving and your brother told us you were going to get help. You've been down lately and we know Bree can be quite harsh. And what we did to those kids, your friends, was so mean; we're sorry. But I want you to know that we'll be here for you." Juniper said with a small smile as Zora returned the smile. With that, the girls all ran to the trap door of the U.S.K.

* * *

"Where are we go... — OMG!" Poppy began to say as she went down the trap door and saw the marvelous cardboard city.

Since it was night-time, most of the cardboard city kids were asleep. This was good. Zora ran towards the town hall with the two girls following behind.

She burst in and with a loud voice, she yelled "Guys, I need your help now. PLEASE!" At first, only silence replied to her demand. But after a few seconds, one of the room doors opened, to show a sleepy Raheem.

"Zora?" He asked with confusion. "Yes, it's me! Could you call up the others? It's an emergency." Zora replied. Raheem didn't wait another second. He quickly knocked on the other U.S.K. kids' doors and woke them up. Soon everybody was out, standing in the main town hall living room with Zora, Poppy, and Juniper standing there too.

What are you doing here?!? What are they doing here?!?" Kamau said angrily. "It's those girls who insulted us! Remember when I told you about them?" Anaya growled. "Well I do." Keesha said through clenched teeth. "We're so sorry! That was — " Poppy began to say, but Zora interrupted. "We don't have time for that now. There's a fire blazing through the town at this very moment!" Zora exclaimed.

The U.S.K kids' eyes popped open but then they recovered from the shock and returned to folding their arms with frowns plastered on their faces.

"And what should we do about it?" Anaya grunted. "The town's gonna burn to the ground, then after that, it's gonna come and burn the U.S.K.!" Zora explained haphazardly. "Oh my..." Keesha said quietly at the realization of what could happen.

Tears started to fill Raheem's eyes as the thought of losing their only home was too much for him to bear. "If we used the golem we could save a few people or —"

"The golem isn't ready. You know that." Keesha interrupted, with worry in her eyes.

"Can't you rush it or something? We don't seem to have any other option." Anaya said in a defeated tone.

"If it were that easy, I'd have done that a long time ago!" Keesha cried. "But maybe... maybe I can try. However, I can't guarantee anything." she warned.

"But it's better to try than to give up entirely." Zora said with a small smile.

Keesha returned a small smile back to her. She then ran to the stairs that went to the lab.

"Okay, here's the plan; Some of you guys, go to the town to make sure everything is still okay there; the rest of you, come with me. I need A LOT of help to get the big guy up and running."

"Good idea. Come to the town square when it's ready, okay? Me and the other girls need to go back; we've left for too long, and we don't want anyone to get suspicious." Zora said. Keesha gave a thumbs up and ran upstairs with Kamau and Anaya.

"I'll come too!" Raheem said, and the four children, Zora, Poppy, Juniper, and Raheem ran outside of the U.S.K., and back into the town that was about to be buried in flames.

Chapter 5

Let's Do This!

"Zora! Oh my goodness where were you?!" her mother cried out as she hugged her really tight.

Zora thought fast; she needed a good excuse. "Uh, one of my friends needed help saving her cat from her house, which was also burning. She turned to Poppy, to verify her story.

"Huh, oh yeah. We managed to save my kitty. She's safe and sound in my younger sister's arms now!" Poppy said with a fake smile.

"Well, I'm glad to hear that!" Zora's mom replied.

At that very moment, heavy footsteps were heard. All the citizens' eyes turned to the direction of a yellow field and out of the shadows walked a large metal beast. Some of the citizens started to scream and confusion filled the air. But Zora smiled and ran up to the beast. "You guys did it! How did you get it up so fast!?" she exclaimed, as three children jumped out of the golem. "Apart from teamwork? Well, while I was frantically setting up the robot, I instantly thought of my dad. He has always told me that the most difficult problems require the calmest of minds, or the issue will never be solved. That has never been truer until this moment, and even though he's gone, I still wanna make him proud." Keesha said with a grin. "Alright, let's get to it!" she said as she and the others were about to jump in the golem again. But at that moment, a woman screamed;

"WAIT! WAIT! My husband and kids are in the forest; they went camping there a few days ago, and they were supposed to be back this afternoon! They could be stuck in the forest, surrounded by fire! Oh, please save them! Save my family!"

"Absolutely! Anaya said as she and the others climbed in the golem. Then, they turned to face the flaming forest.

* * *

"I see them!" After what felt like hours during this desperate time, Raheem pointed to an area near a cliff that was about to be engulfed by the flames, with three people screaming and waving their hands frantically in the air.

"If that's not them, I must be a monkey's aunty!" Anaya said with a chuckle as Keesha used the golem's hands to scoop up the people and let them inside. In jumped a man, who appeared to be hurt a bit, and two children, a boy and a girl. The children were no older than eight and had fear swimming in their eyes. "We've got this!" Raheem said as he brought out the first aid kit that hung in the safety cabinet of the golem, while Juniper and Poppy calmed down the two children.

The little boy was sobbing quietly. "I knew I shouldn't have been playing with that lighter, this is all my fault!" he mumbled as tears streaked down his face, while the two girls looked cautiously at him.

Meanwhile, Zora and the U.S.K. (with the exception of Raheem) were at the control panel, deciding their next move. They were surrounded by the fire and it was reaching more parts of the town. What were they going to do now? At that moment, Kamau spotted a large lake not far from them. "Look guys. water!"

"The place we go swimming!" Anaya said excitedly.

As they moved the golem towards it, Zora furrowed her eyebrows. "How are we gonna transport the water to the flames?" she asked.

"We could... dig a path from it to run down towards the town?" Anaya suggested.

"It'll take too long," Kamau said.

"He's right, and time is the last thing we have right now. Besides, it could flood the town."

That was when Keesha's eyes lit up. "OH MY GOODNESS! HOW COULD I FORGET?! she said enthusiastically. She pushed a button and the golem's arms turned into what seemed like cannons, then it bent over and started to suck up water from the lake.

"Remember when Anaya said we should get water guns to play with next time we all went swimming together? Well, I had added a water gun feature to the golem not too long after!" she said with a grin as her friend jumped with glee. The golem stopped sucking up water and turned to face the forest. "Hasta la vista, fuego!" Kamau said as Keesha activated the spray, dowsing the forest with a rain-like shower. The flames subsided and the golem moved towards the town, doing the same to the houses and buildings. The flames slowly disappeared and a shout of jubilee and praise escaped from the townspeople.

Zora smiled. Kamau smirked. Keesha chuckled. Anaya grinned. Raheem clapped.

The U.S.K. had done it; they saved the entire town!

* * *

Everyone was really grateful to the U.S.K. for saving their little town. The kids got interviewed several times and even had a statue of the golem built in the middle of town to show their appreciation. The U.S.K. were getting their own moment of fame! The townspeople even wanted the U.S.K to live in the town they helped save, but the U.S.K kids politely declined the offer. They had grown attached to their lovely underground home. However, since they chose to still live in the old but cozy abandoned factory, the mayor took her appreciation a step further and assured them that the U.S.K will no longer be bothered by city officials and demolition workers, meaning that the little community could continue living there in peace. Many people also offered gifts to the U.S.K., like brand new toys, clothes, food, and much more cool stuff and even though they did not live there, they were always welcomed in the town. Life was more than better for them.

* * *

"So... I never properly apologized to you guys." Zora said as she sat on the deck with Kamau, as Keesha, Raheem and Anaya were splashing in the lake and the iron golem playfully sprayed them with water.

Kamau pretended to think. "You know, now that I think about it; you never did." He said with a playful scoff.

Zora smirked a bit. "I'm sorry, I really am. I let the fame get to my head and forgot the good times and fun you guys brought to me. You all mean a lot to me and it was dumb of me to abandon you like that... I'm such a loser." She said sadly.

"You really are," Kamau said, fighting back a grin.

"Hey! You're supposed to say 'Oh no, don't say that! You're not a loser!' Where's the moral support!" she complained with a laugh.

"Oh yeah, it's right...here!" He screamed as he pushed Zora into the lake.

She resurfaced, laughing as the other kids did the same. "Okay, I deserved that!" She said with a smile. Kamau grinned before getting up and running forward to perform a cannon ball, which covered his friends in water. Especially Zora. "Oh my goodness! I've suffered enough!" She said, still laughing.

"Have you?" Keesha said mischievously, as she and the rest started to splash Zora with more water. She also splashed them and soon, the kids were playing gleefully in the water, as laughter and enjoyment filled the air.

"You're one of us, Zora. You always have been." Keesha said, as Zora beamed with a wide smile. This was it. This was what she truly wanted. And she was beyond happy now.

About the Author

Sophie Eruokwu lives in Saint John, New Brunswick with her family and she is currently a grade 12 student attending Saint John High School. She likes to read, write, draw, and create stories in her head.

She hopes to be a successful author amongst other things in the future.